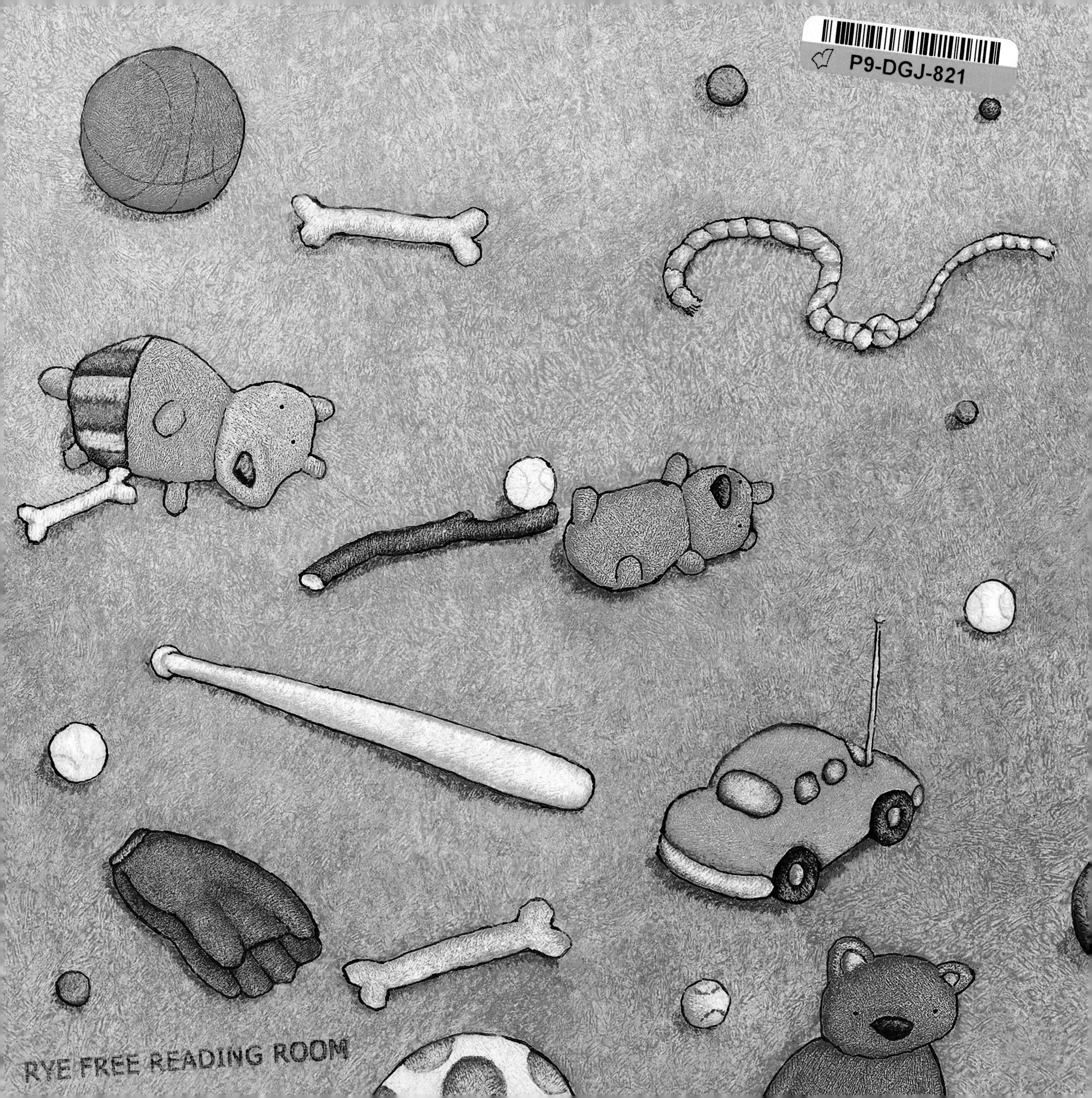
P9-DGJ-821
RYE FREE READING ROOM

For My Very Own Father — who, if he were a dog, would of course be a most intelligent, witty, and dignified breed
E. B.

For Dad, of course! And the dogs, as with every dog I have ever drawn, are for Mom.
R. C.

Special thanks to the ever-cheerful, patient, wise Joan Powers — and to Randy Hilarious Artist Cecil, to Liza, Anita, Kate, Elise, Ellen, Phyllis, Jane, the Zoo, Liz, Tiff, Will, and Jake, and most of all to cheerleader Josie, the Rose Princess.

First edition 2006

Library of Congress Cataloging-in-Publication Data

Bluemle, Elizabeth.
My father the dog / Elizabeth Bluemle ; illustrated by Randy Cecil. — 1st ed.
p. cm.
Summary: A young girl suspects that her father is really a dog because he performs such acts as fetching the newspaper and chasing balls.
ISBN 0-7636-2222-2
[1. Dogs — Fiction. 2. Fathers — Fiction.] I. Cecil, Randy, ill. II. Title.
PZ7.B625254Myf 2006
[E] — dc22   2005054285

4 6 8 10 9 7 5 3

Printed in China

This book was typeset in SoupBone.
The illustrations were done in oil.

Candlewick Press
2067 Massachusetts Avenue
Cambridge, Massachusetts 02140

visit us at www.candlewick.com

My Father the Dog

Elizabeth Bluemle illustrated by Randy Cecil

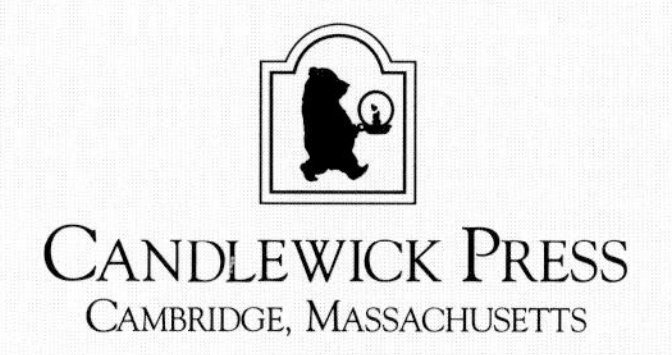

CANDLEWICK PRESS
CAMBRIDGE, MASSACHUSETTS

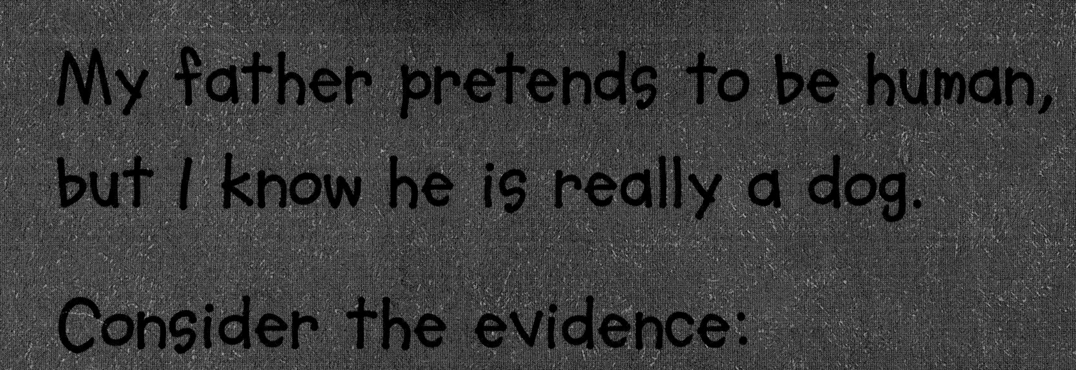

My father pretends to be human,
but I know he is really a dog.

Consider the evidence:

When he wakes up, he's fuzzy around the edges.
He starts off the day with a good scratch.

He fetches the newspaper every morning.

My father loves to roughhouse and play tug of war.

He hates to lose.

In the car, he likes the windows down
and a breeze on his face.

He has been known to use a tree for a quick pit stop.

My father can lie around for hours.

He growls when you startle him out of a nap.

If you throw a ball, he'll chase after it.

My father loves snacks.

I've never actually seen him begging for scraps under the kitchen table, but it could happen.

When he toots, he looks around
the room like someone else did it.

He is good at looking innocent when
he knows he's done something wrong.

If he hears a noise in the middle of the night,
he runs downstairs to investigate.

My father is loyal and thinks we're the best family in the world . . .

which is good, ’cause Mom says we can keep him.

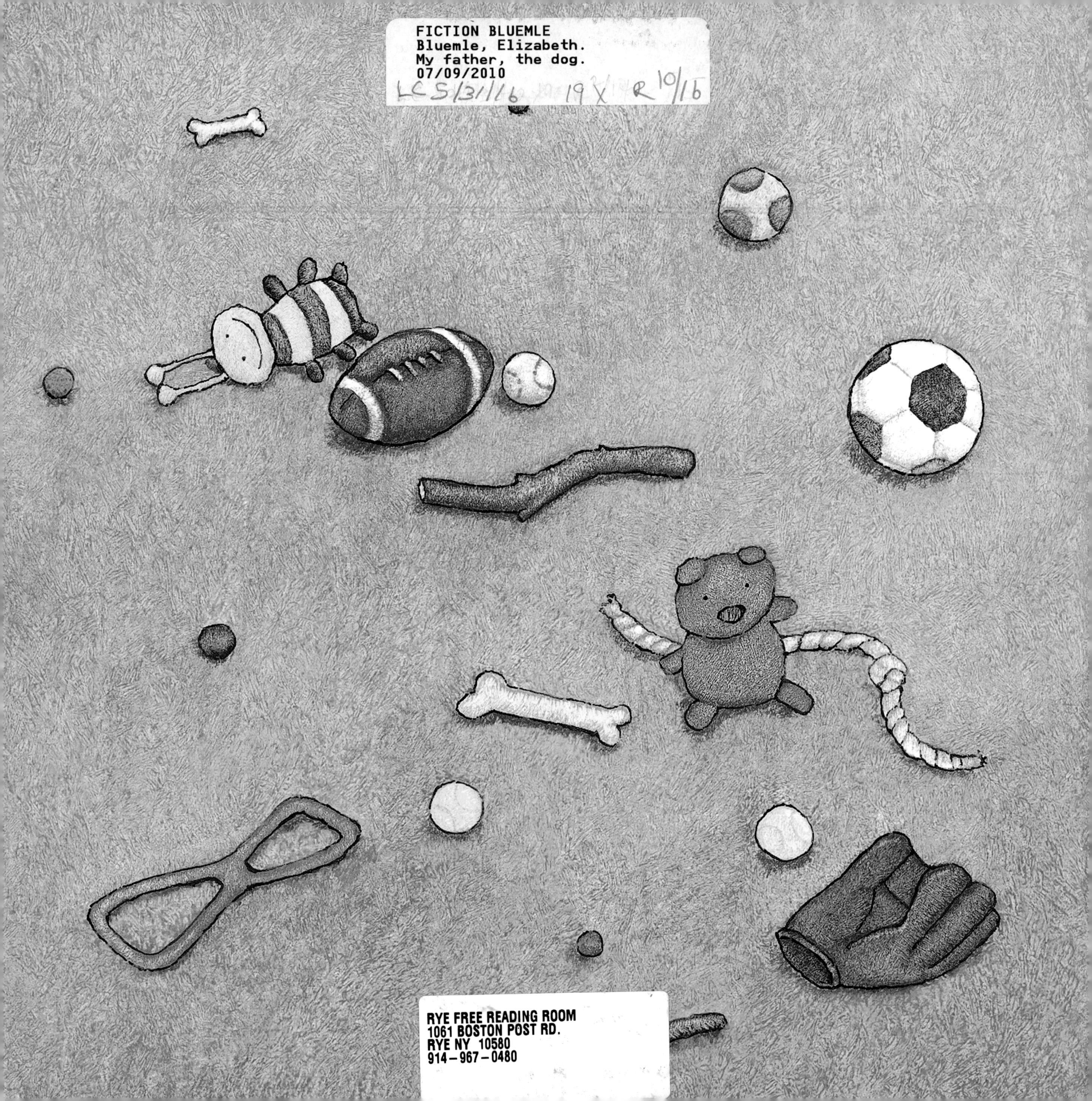